Dear Parent:

Congratulations! Your child is taking the first steps on an exciting journey. The destination? Independent reading!

STEP INTO READING® will help your child get there. The program offers five steps to reading success. Each step includes fun stories and colorful art. There are also Step into Reading Sticker Books, Step into Reading Math Readers, Step into Reading Write-In Readers, Step into Reading Phonics Readers, and Step into Reading Phonics First Steps! Boxed Sets—a complete literacy program with something for every child.

Learning to Read, Step by Step!

Ready to Read Preschool–Kindergarten
• big type and easy words • rhyme and rhythm • picture clues
For children who know the alphabet and are eager to begin reading.

Reading with Help Preschool–Grade 1
• basic vocabulary • short sentences • simple stories
For children who recognize familiar words and sound out new words with help.

Reading on Your Own Grades 1–3
• engaging characters • easy-to-follow plots • popular topics
For children who are ready to read on their own.

Reading Paragraphs Grades 2–3
• challenging vocabulary • short paragraphs • exciting stories
For newly independent readers who read simple sentences with confidence.

Ready for Chapters Grades 2–4
• chapters • longer paragraphs • full-color art
For children who want to take the plunge into chapter books but still like colorful pictures.

STEP INTO READING® is designed to give every child a successful reading experience. The grade levels are only guides. Children can progress through the steps at their own speed, developing confidence in their reading, no matter what their grade.

Remember, a lifetime love of reading starts with a single step!

To Kayla
—N.E.

Sushi Pack™ and related trademarks © 2009 Cloudco, Inc. Used under license by Random House, Inc. All rights reserved. Published in the United States by Random House Children's Books, a division of Random House, Inc., 1745 Broadway, New York, NY 10019, and in Canada by Random House of Canada Limited, Toronto.

Step into Reading, Random House, and the Random House colophon are registered trademarks of Random House, Inc.

Visit us on the Web!
www.stepintoreading.com
www.randomhouse.com/kids

Educators and librarians, for a variety of teaching tools, visit us at
www.randomhouse.com/teachers

Library of Congress Cataloging-in-Publication Data
Eliopulos, Nick.
Double trouble / by Eliopulos, Nick; illustrated by Carlos Villagra.
— 1st ed.
    p.   cm. — (Step into reading. A Step 2 book.)
ISBN: 978-0-375-85212-1 (trade pbk.)
ISBN: 978-0-375-95212-8 (lib. bdg.)
PZ7.E417 Dou 2008 [E]—dc22 2007041754

Printed in the United States of America   10 9 8 7 6 5 4 3 2 1   First Edition

Double Trouble

By Nick Eliopulos

Illustrated by Carlos Villagra

Based on the episode "Wassup Wasabi?"
by Tom Ruegger and Nicholas Hollander

Random House 🏠 New York

The Sushi Pack
were
super heroes.

Ikura

Maguro

Tako

Kani

Wasabi

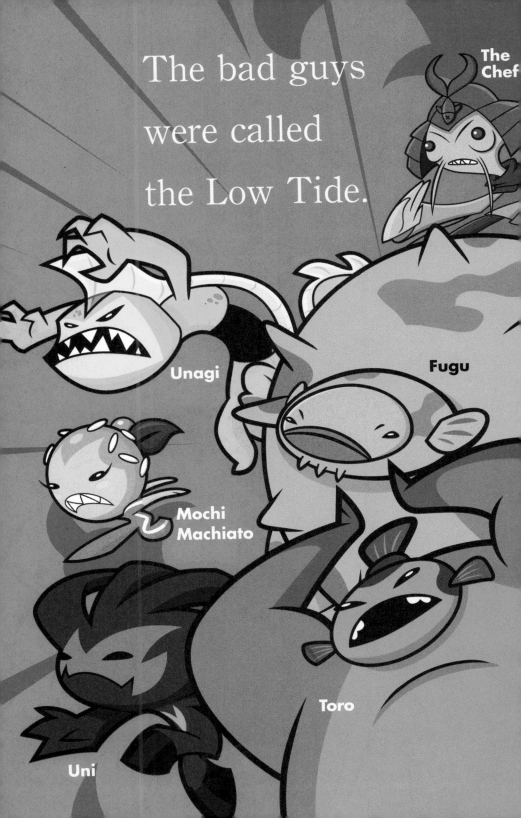

The Sushi Pack
fought
the Low Tide!

Wasabi faced Toro.
Toro was much bigger
than Wasabi.

Wasabi was not afraid.

He pushed Toro over.

The Sushi Pack won!

Wasabi was a hero.

He was even on TV!

Wasabi's friends
teased him.
Wasabi cried
and ran away.

Wasabi's friends
did not mean
to make him sad.
They went to find him.

12

But the bad Chef
and the Low Tide
found Wasabi first!

The Chef
put Wasabi
in a cold chair
made of ice.

Then he stole some of
Wasabi's green flame.

The Chef
mixed the green flame
with some spices.
He made
Fake Wasabi!

19

Wasabi was worried
about his friends.
Fake Wasabi
might trick them!

He pulled extra hard
and broke free
from the ice chair!

The Sushi Pack

saw their friend.

They ran toward him.

But it was Fake Wasabi.
He threw
green fireballs at them!

Wasabi came to help.
"Two Wasabis?" asked
Maguro.

They did not know
which Wasabi was real!

Then Tako had an idea.
"We should say
we are sorry!"
he said.

The Sushi Pack
turned to
both Wasabis.
"We're sorry," they said.

The real Wasabi
hugged his
friends.

All alone,
Fake Wasabi
turned into
a pile of spices!

The Sushi Pack
was back together!
They chased
the Low Tide
out of town.

Maguro said,
"New rule:
No more teasing!"
Wasabi smiled.
He was glad to have
such good friends!